MW00953540
Isadora and the sloppy dragon

To everyone who's had trouble finding their voice.

Isadorn the Unicorn and the Sloppy Dragon

Written by Angela Castillo

Illustrations by Indira Zuleta

Printed in the United States of America

First Edition, 2019 ISBN 9781710079784

Isadorn the Unicorn and the Sloppy Dragon

Angela Castillo

Isadorn the unicorn lived in a lovely waterfall grotto with beautiful flower bushes. Everything was perfect.

One day, a dragon named Dunfer moved into the cave next door. At first, Dunfer seemed nice. He waved and smiled a goofy dragon smile. But it didn't stay that way for long.

Piles of broken treasure and jewels filled Dunfer's front yard.

Dunfer made snarling, gnarling noises day and night that shook his whole cave.

Isadorn tried putting cloud fluff over her head,
but it messed up her mane.

"I'm tired of seeing the clutter," Isadorn told her best friend, Lema, the water sprite.
"Hmmm." Lema tapped her chin.
"Why not talk to Dunfer and tell him how you feel?"

Isadorn shook her silky mane. "What if I make him mad? He might yell at me! What if I make him sad? He might cry boiling dragon tears."

The next morning when Dunfer came outside, he burped an earth-shaking burp. A giant ball of fire flew from his jaws and burnt Isadorn's favorite rose bush to the ground.

"That's it!" Isadorn said to Lema. "I've had it with that dragon! He makes me so mad!" She pawed at the ground, sending up glittery showers of sparkles.

"What happened now?" Lema asked.

"Dunfer burnt down my roses."

"You have to talk to him." Lema said.

"No," said Isadorn. "What if he gets mad? What if I hurt his feelings?"

"But he's made you angry," Lema said gently. "Your feelings matter too. If you let that anger boil inside, it will only hurt you more."

Isadorn took deep breaths so she could calm down.
She wrote out all the words she wanted to say.

She practiced in a mirror.
She even practiced in the shower.
Finally, she was ready.

The next evening, she knocked on
Dunfer's door with a trembling hoof.

She wanted to run away, but she gathered her
courage. "He needs to know how I feel."

Dunfer came to the door with his same goofy grin.

"Hello, Isadorn. What a pleasant surprise!"

Isadorn looked into his golden dragon eyes and gulped.

"What if he's mad? What if he gets sad?"

But she shook her mane and remembered
what she'd practiced.

"Dunfer, I'm not getting sleep at night because you make so much noise.

I'm feeling sad because you burnt down my favorite flower bush, and didn't even say you were sorry!

When I see your messy yard, it makes me feel sad. Do you think I could help you clean it up?"

Dunfer's smile wavered a bit. "Oh no." He stepped out of his cave and peered around. "the yard is a bit messy, isn't it? Fire and fiddlesticks, I did burn down your flower bush. I'm truly sorry, Isadorn. Please forgive me."

Suddenly, Isadorn felt light as a fairy. "Of course, I forgive you, Dunfer. Could we be friends?"
"Sure!" Dunfer's grin was back. "Shall we go search for a new flower bush in the woods?"

So the two new friends went off together.

With Lema's help, they planted a beautiful bush of rainbow roses.

Dunfer and Isadorn cleaned up all the broken treasure and put a fountain in Dunfer's front yard.

The snarling, gnarling noise turned out to be dragon laughter. Dunfer promised not to read dragon joke books late at night so Isadorn could get her beauty rest.

And Isadorn was glad she decided to tell how she felt. It was much better than having that bubbling brewing anger inside.

Not only that, but she was happy to have made a friend.

the End.

What to do if someone hurts your feelings.

Wait until you're calm. If you speak up when you're mad and upset, you might say something you didn't mean to. Give yourself some time to cool down and think about what you need to say.

Think of kind words. Don't be harsh when you talk to someone about how you were hurt. Speak to them the way you would want to be spoken to.

Practice. Just like Isadorn, you should practice what to say. If you like, ask an adult to help you think of the right words.

Learn how to use "I" statements. For example: "I feel sad when you take my toy. Could you please ask nicely to make sure I'm finished with it?" Or, "I get upset when you call me that name. Could you please call me (name) instead?"

Listen to what the other person says. They might not have even realized they hurt your feelings.

Prepare. Even if the other person does get mad or sad, it's still good to tell them how you feel. They might even think about it and try harder to treat someone else better the next time. You never know what tiny seeds of truth and kindness can do!

Question time!

Do you think Isadorn did the right thing by talking to Dunfer when she was sad?

Why or why not?

Have you ever been mad at someone?

Did you try to talk to them about it?

Do you think you could try the same steps Isadorn used to decide what to say when someone makes you sad or mad?

Find out more about Angela Castillo and her books for kids at

http://tobythetrilby.weebly.com.
You can also find all her books on Amazon.com in paperback and Kindle.

Find these other great books by the author on Amazon!

Made in the USA
Lexington, KY
08 December 2019